W9-CMF-583

Pandarella

written by Charlotte Guillain ☆ illustrated by Dawn Beacon

Raintree

Chicago, Illinois

© 2013 Raintree
an imprint of Capstone Global Library, LLC
Chicago, Illinois

To contact Capstone Global Library please phone 800-747-4992, or visit our website
www.capstonepub.com

Edited by Daniel Nunn, Rebecca Rissman, and Sian Smith
Designed by Joanna Hinton-Malivoire
Original illustrations © Capstone Global Library, Ltd., 2013
Illustrated by Dawn Beacon
Production by Victoria Fitzgerald
Originated by Capstone Global Library, Ltd.
Printed in China

16 15 14 13 12
10 9 8 7 6 5 4 3 2 1

Library of Congress Cataloging-in-Publication Data
Guillain, Charlotte.
  Pandarella / Charlotte Guillain.
    p. cm. -- (Animal fairy tales)
Summary: A simplified version of the familiar fairy tale featuring a panda who, with help
from her furry godmother, attends a ball and dances with a handsome prince. Includes a
note on the history of the tale.
  ISBN 978-1-4109-5025-3 (hb) -- ISBN 978-1-4109-5031-4 (pb) -- ISBN 978-1-4109-5043-7
(big book) [1. Fairy tales. 2. Folklore--France.] I. Perrault, Charles, 1628-1703. Cendrillon.
English. II. Title.

PZ8.G947Pan 2013
398.2—dc23   2012017423
[E]

Every effort has been made to contact copyright holders of material reproduced in
this book. Any omissions will be rectified in subsequent printings if notice is given to
the publisher.

Characters

Pandarella

stepmother and
two stepsisters

Furry Godmother

prince

messenger

Once upon a time, there lived a beautiful panda called Pandarella. She lived with her stepmother and two stepsisters. They were very unkind and made her do all the work in the house.

One day, a messenger brought an invitation from the royal palace. The prince had invited them all to a ball.

But the stepsisters told Pandarella she could not go.

Pandarella's stepmother and stepsisters
got dressed up and went to the ball.

When they had gone, Pandarella sat
down and began to cry. Suddenly,
there was a flash of light and her
Furry Godmother appeared.

"Don't cry, Pandarella!" said the Furry Godmother. "You **shall** go to the ball!" She waved her magic wand and suddenly Pandarella was wearing a beautiful dress and delicate glass slippers.

Pandarella's stepmother and stepsisters
got dressed up and went to the ball.

When they had gone, Pandarella sat
down and began to cry. Suddenly,
there was a flash of light and her
Furry Godmother appeared.

The Furry Godmother waved her wand again and a carriage and horses appeared! They were ready to take Pandarella to the ball.

"Make sure you come home before the clock strikes midnight," she warned Pandarella.

When Pandarella got to the ball, the prince couldn't take his eyes off her. They danced together for hours. Suddenly, the clock began to chime midnight. The magic was about to wear off!

Pandarella ran away as fast as she could.
But as she ran, one of her glass slippers
fell to the ground.

The prince picked up the slipper. He didn't
know who Pandarella was, but he knew
the slipper would fit her. He decided to
search the land until he found her.

Before long, the prince's search
took him to Pandarella's house.
Her stepsisters tried to cram their
paws into the slipper, but they were
the wrong shape.

Then the prince spotted Pandarella,
and asked her to try the slipper on.

It fit her perfectly!

The prince and Pandarella went to
the palace, where they were married.
Pandarella never had to work for
her stepsisters again, and she lived
happily ever after.

The end

Where does this story come from?

You've probably already heard the story that *Pandarella* is based on—*Cinderella*. There are many different versions of this story. When people tell a story, they often make little changes to make it their own. How would you change this story?

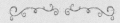

The history of the story

The *Cinderella* story was first written down by the Brothers Grimm. Jacob (1785–1863) and Wilhelm (1786–1859) Grimm lived near the city of Frankfurt, in Germany. They collected and wrote down many fairy stories and folktales. These tales were told by oral storytellers who entertained people in the days before radio and television.

The original story is called *Ashputtel*. A girl's mother dies and her father remarries. His new wife has two daughters who make the girl work in the kitchen and call her Ashputtel (Cinderella) because she is always dirty from the ashes in the fire. Her father brings her a hazel twig, which she plants at her mother's grave. It grows into a tree and a bird nests there.

Then, the two sisters are asked to a royal ball. Ashputtel begs her stepmother to let her go, too. The stepmother throws out a plate of peas and says Ashputtel can go if she picks up all the peas. The birds help Ashputtel pick up the peas, but her stepmother still refuses to let her go. Ashputtel is left behind and sits crying under the hazel tree.

Suddenly, a bird flies down and gives her a gold and silver dress and silk slippers. Ashputtel goes to the ball and nobody recognizes her. She dances with the prince but runs away and hides at the end of the night. The prince follows her but cannot find the girl he danced with. This happens again on the second night, and on the third night Ashputtel leaves a slipper as she runs away. The prince takes the slipper to her home, and one sister cuts off her toe so the slipper will fit! As the prince takes her home, a bird sings to him to go back. Then the second sister squeezes her foot in and the prince starts to take her home. Again, the bird warns him it's a trick. Then he sees Ashputtel by the hazel tree. She tries on the slipper, and the prince takes her away to his palace.